# Super Scar

by Melanie Tucker

Illustrated by Ricky Audi

For Seth, Levi, and Asher

There once was a boy who was
born with a special heart.

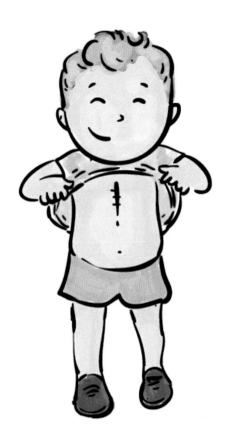

He had surgery when he was little
that left a super scar on his chest.

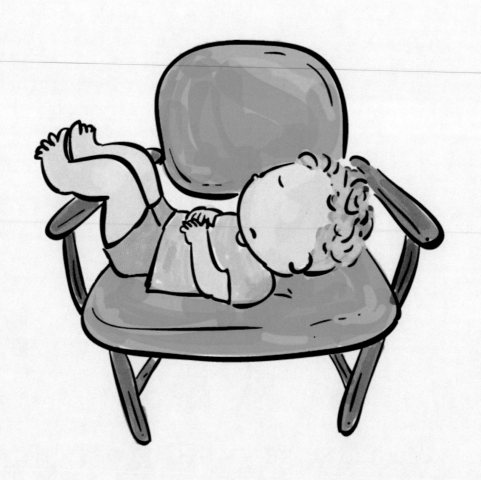

Sometimes he felt tired and had to rest.

Sometimes he couldn't keep up with his friends,

even though he tried his very best.

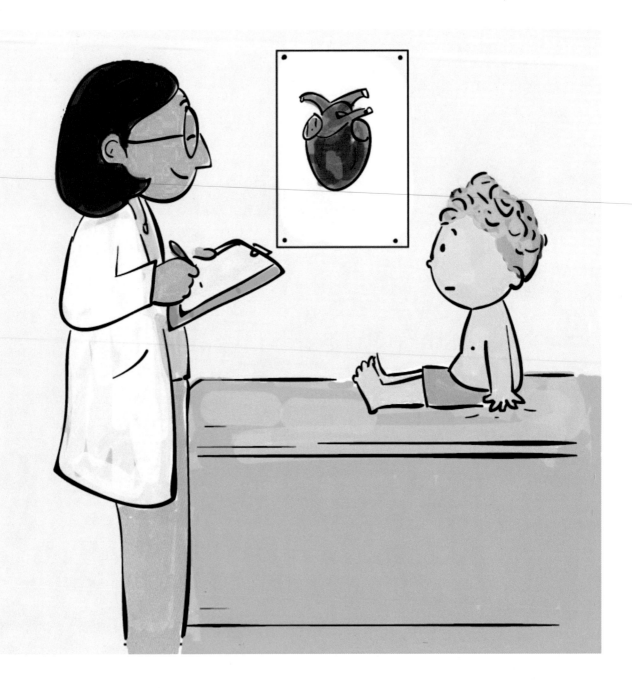

Sometimes he had to go to a special doctor to check his special heart,

even stay overnight in the hospital.

But whenever he was feeling scared,

he would look at his super scar.

It reminded him of how super brave,

and super strong,

and super special he was,

and that he could handle anything!

Made in the USA
Las Vegas, NV
21 January 2024